# The Lion
## and
# The Mouse

CAROL JONES

*For my niece Meghann Elizabeth*
*with love ~ C.J.*

First American edition 1997
Originally published in Australia by HarperCollins*Publishers* Pty
Limited as an Angus & Robertson book

Walter Lorraine (wr) Books

For information about this and other Houghton Mifflin trade
and reference books and multimedia products, visit The Bookstore
at Houghton Mifflin on the World Wide Web at
http://www.hmco.com/trade/.

Printed in Hong Kong

10 9 8 7 6 5 4 3 2 1

# The Lion
## and
# The Mouse

CAROL JONES

Houghton Mifflin Company
Boston

One afternoon, Mouse was looking for some adventure. He was bored with playing chase and hide 'n' seek with his brothers and sisters among the sacks of flour and barrels of oranges. Mouse was curious about life outside his quiet home in the hold of the sailing ship, the *Indiana*.

"I'm off to do some exploring," he called, jumping onto the staircase rail that led up to the ship's deck.

"Oh, do be careful!" pleaded one of his younger sisters. "Mother has warned us about the many dangers above."

"Yes, you could be a nice snack for a hungry cat," said his eldest sister, trying to frighten her adventurous brother.

But Mouse wasn't listening. He had already scampered up the rail and disappeared from view.

It was dusk when Mouse squeezed through a crack and found himself on the top-most deck. His heart thumped with excitement but he was unaware of the silent figure stalking him. It was Ship's Cat.

Suddenly, Cat pounced. Mouse scampered desperately trying to escape but Cat's paw flicked his back legs and Mouse found himself falling, falling, falling …

SPLASH!

Frantically Mouse pumped his tiny legs in the cold ocean trying to stay afloat. A piece of wood brushed by his head and, thankful, he dragged himself onto it.

Throughout the night Mouse lay cold and trembling on his tiny raft and thought of his mother and father and brothers and sisters who would be safely snuggled up behind the flour sacks.

"I wish I was as brave as a lion," he thought.

At sunrise, Mouse was still huddled on his makeshift raft as it bobbled on the ocean currents but his spirits were lifted by the sight of a beach ahead. Soon a big rolling wave arrived. It picked up the raft and Mouse enjoyed a thrilling surf all the way to the shore.

Mouse rose unsteadily to his feet. His legs felt wobbly but he was grateful to be on land, and now he desperately needed a drink.

"I hope I receive a friendly welcome," murmured Mouse to himself. But as he trudged up the beach, two hermit crabs crawled menacingly out of a rock pool, snapping their pincers at the new arrival.

"Get lost!" squeaked Mouse indignantly, and he whisked his tail out of reach.

Meanwhile, in the middle of the steamy jungle, Lion let out a thunderous roar. Monkeys stopped chattering, parrots ceased squawking and even snakes halted their hissing.

Lion gave a satisfied, pompous smile, yawned sleepily and settled down for his afternoon nap.

The jungle animals went quietly
back to their business.
No one dared disturb
Lion, the mighty
King of the Jungle.

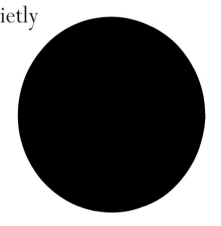

autiously, Mouse made his way up the beach and into the jungle
with its towering trees and tangled vines. To his delight, he found
flowing stream and Mouse sipped the cool, fresh water taking a rest on
hat he thought was a log. Suddenly, Mouse found himself sliding off and
azing up at gaping jaws and huge sharp teeth.

Iow nice, a lovely furry snack,"
loated Crocodile.

rozen with fear,
Mouse shut his eyes.

NAP!

rocodile's jaws slammed
hut! But Mouse only felt a
ainful tug on his tail and when he dared to open his eyes,
e found himself whizzing upwards through the air.

second or two later Mouse was perched on the branch
f a tree and gazing across at the cheeky face of Monkey.

"Th-th-thank you for saving my life," stammered Mouse, who was recovering from his narrow escape.

"Think nothing of it," chortled Monkey, cracking a nut and handing it to Mouse. "Welcome to the jungle. I watched you arrive, and your surfing is sensational!"

Mouse nibbled gratefully at the nut. He had found a friend and was feeling better already.

"Now, hop on my back and I'll take you home to meet my family," invited Monkey.

So, with Mouse perched on his back, Monkey went swinging through the trees towards his home by the banana palms. Unfortunately, Mouse found himself slipping off Monkey's back and falling down, down, down through the canopy of leaves towards the ground …

. . . **r**ight onto the nose of Lion, the King of the Jungle!

Lion, who had been sleeping peacefully, awoke suddenly, letting out an angry roar. His huge paw clamped down upon Mouse and held him prisoner.

Mouse looked up towards the trees but Monkey had disappeared unaware that he had lost his new friend.

Lion roared again. 'How dare you wake me. Your impudent mistake will cost you your life!" he growled, and opened his huge jaws to swallow the tiny Mouse.

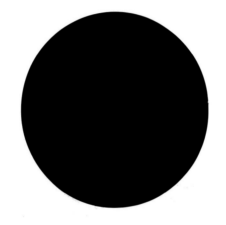

Just in time, Mouse discovered his voice. "P-p-please don't eat me Mighty Lion," he begged. "I really didn't mean to wake you. I'm new around here and it was an accident that I slipped off Monkey's back. I promise it won't ever happen again."

Lion was unmoved. "Well, I'm still going to eat you. You have spoiled my afternoon nap."

"Please don't, your Majesty. If you spare my humble life I'll promise to repay your favor," Mouse pleaded bravely. "Small creatures are capable of great deeds."

Lion threw back his head with laughter. "What an incredible idea," he declared. "How could a tiny mouse help me, the undisputed King of the Jungle? Still, I admire your courage. You are a brave little fellow, so I'm going to set you free. Off with you before I change my mind," said Lion.

Mouse decided that he should find Monkey as the jungle was no safe place for a tiny mouse on his own. But after walking for many hours with no sign of his friend, Mouse's legs were very tired. He climbed a tree and began practicing swinging on a vine like Monkey had done and soon Mouse was gliding through the trees just like his friend.

Swinging over a waterhole, Mouse lost his grip and once again went plunging down through the air. Fortunately this time, he stuck out his tail, curled it around a branch and saved himself from falling into the mouth of Hippopotamus who was enjoying a bath with her family.

That night, alone in the jungle, Mouse sheltered in the fork of a tree and tried to shut out the scary sounds.

"I've really had enough of adventure. I want to go home," he thought.

When Mouse awoke next morning he found himself staring across at Python who was writhing around the tree, baring his fangs ready to swallow Mouse in one gulp.

But Mouse after so many narrow escapes had learned to be a fast mover and used his new-found aerial skills to swing out of Python's way.

"I don't intend to be anyone's meal," he scolded.

Resting safely on another branch, Mouse pricked up his ears at a sound like thunder. Then he realized that it was the angry, unhappy roar of Lion; a roar that Mouse recognized as a cry for help.

Remembering his promise to the King of the Jungle, and without a thought for his own safety, Mouse scuttled out of the tree and raced off in the direction of the sound.

ouse fought his way through the tangled undergrowth of the jungle until he arrived at a clearing. Here he could see Lion ensnared in a large net. Lion was thrashing about, straining himself against the thick ropes, but the hunters' trap had been well set and the King of the Jungle struggled in vain.

Venturing closer, Mouse could see how bedraggled and unhappy Lion looked, so different from the sleek and proud King of the Jungle whom Mouse had met the day before.

Lion looked down at Mouse. "Why are you here tiny Mouse? Have you come to tease me about my fate?" he asked with tears filling his eyes.

"Of course not," said Mouse indignantly. "I've come to set you free!"

Immediately Mouse set to work. With his sharp teeth he began to gnaw at one of the thick ropes. Progress was slow but Mouse diligently stuck to his task.

When the first rope fell apart, Lion gave a little roar of surprise. "I do believe this little fellow may be able to help me," he said.

Mouse worked steadily on, encouraged by Monkey, Parrot, and the other jungle animals who had arrived to watch.

For a long time Mouse nibbled at the net until, finally, he had succeeded in gnawing through enough ropes to enable Lion to be set free.

As soon as he burst out of the net, Lion celebrated his freedom with the mightiest roar ever heard in the jungle. Then Lion came forward to thank his rescuer.

T hank you, little friend. You have saved my life," he said. "Small creatures *are* capable of great deeds. You should never fear danger in this jungle again as I will always be your protector," promised Lion with great sincerity.

Mouse's whiskers twitched with pride. "I appreciate your promise but I really just want to return to my home on the ship," he replied modestly.

Parrot told Lion that he had seen the *Indiana* anchored in a nearby bay and Lion offered to take Mouse home.

"Hop onto my back, little friend," invited Lion crouching down. "I know how to get you home."

So, Mouse climbed with a farewell gift from Parrot onto Lion's broad, golden back. Then Lion padded through the jungle on his way to the seashore.

On their arrival, Lion strode down to the water's edge where he let out three majestic roars and, to Mouse's amazement, a green turtle emerged from the sea. Wide-eyed, Mouse listened as Lion arranged his transport back to the ship.

"Your little friend will be safe with me," said Turtle. "And he won't even get his feet wet!"

Perched proudly on the sturdy back of Turtle, Mouse waved goodbye to his jungle friends and headed out to sea.

Turtle rowed slowly and gracefully and when he reached the ship, Mouse jumped nimbly onto the anchor chain.

Mouse breathed a sigh of relief! He was home and he couldn't wait to tell his brothers and sisters of his new friends and his adventures with Lion — the King of the Jungle.

One Good Deed * Deserves Another *